DISCARD

Published by Simian Books LLC
304 West Gardenia Drive,
Phoenix, AZ 85021

USA

First Edition 2017

Library of Congress
Control Number 2017902015
Michael Hale, author, illustrator
Bad Monkey Business 32 p.

Manufactured in China
ISBN 978-0692-84542-4
10 9 8 7 6 5 4 3 2 1

Design by Michael Hale

For Austin, Carter
and all of my friends
at the Zoo.

Bad Monkey Business

Written & Illustrated by Michael Hale

On a rainy, rainy day in her house on the hill,

Mrs. J.C. McGoody had started to fill
a cup with some tea, after mopping the floor...
When she heard a faint knock come from her front door.

She opened the door and to her surprise
stood a very wet monkey of very small size.

"Can I help you?" she asked,
in a voice soft and sweet,
as the monkey barged in
without wiping his feet.

He dragged in a rope, to which something was tied
and she got quite a scare when it wandered inside.

She picked up a chair to keep the lion at bay
when she noticed the monkey was running away.

But he ran straight ahead, ignoring her words.

Then he opened the windows
and in came the birds.

The room filled with birds all squawking and flying,
while Mrs. McGoody, was running and trying
to catch that small monkey and trying quite hard...

But he jumped through the window,
down to the back yard.

Where he unlatched and opened
her old cellar door
and went back in the house,
where he was just before.

She ran fast to catch him, quick down the stairs,
past the beast in her parlor, asleep on her chairs,

to the door of the basement,
near the clock on the wall.
But just as she got there...
something started to crawl.

The door started shaking. Then burst open wide.
And out came the monkey not trying to hide...

But riding on top of a giant green snake!
A constrictor so big, you might think it was fake.

The back kitchen door was broken in half
as a rhino charged in with a slouching giraffe.

On their heels came a zebra, a tiger, a bear,
and somehow an elephant squeezed inside there.

She cried, "Stop you bad monkey!
Can you hear what I say?
That's enough of this
bad monkey business today!"

But that monkey let in
even more than before...
when another faint knock
came from the front door.

"Please, please go away!"
She started to sob.
But when it opened this time,
it was Zookeeper Bob.

He ran to the monkey who jumped to his arm.

"You did it! They're here! You saved them from harm!"

"All of this rain caused a flood at the zoo!
The water was rising. Oh, what could we do?!

This quick thinking monkey had a very good plan.
He opened the gates and out they all ran...

He led them all here.
To safe, higher ground.

Down in the flooding,
they all might have drowned."

In her house on the hill
when the rain finally stopped,

Mrs. J.C. McGoody went back in and mopped.
Her floors and her rooms cleaned up nice as can be.

And when it was done, had a nice cup of tea.